WELL, *SOMEONE'S* DOING ALL THIS MISCHIEF!

"I knew it, I knew it!" shrieked Tiffany. "There's some kind of maniac loose in school!"

"Oh, for pete's sake," said Diego in disgust. "I'm sorry I said anything."

"No! I know I'm right!" Tiffany's eyes were wide with terror. "It's the shredder," she said in a quavering voice. "It's going through the school attacking things. First Mrs. Doubleday's scarf. Then the anteater stuffing. Then Mrs. Doubleday's papers and the phone cord. Then the rope. And I bet—I bet he's going to start in on us next!"

Look for these other LUNCHROOM titles:

RUBBERBAND STEW

Ann Hodgman

Illustrated by Roger Leyonmark

SPLASH™

B

A BERKLEY / SPLASH BOOK

Chapter One

A Lunchtime Surprise

"Hand me that broom, will you, Bob?" asked Bonnie Kirk. "I need to sweep up a broken head over here."

"Just a sec," replied her friend Bob Kelly. "Let me dump this pirates' gold first." Carefully he carried a dustpan brimming with fake pieces of eight over to the trash can and tipped it in. Then he picked up the broom and carried it over to Bonnie. "Here you go," he said.

"Thanks."

Bonnie, Bob, and the rest of their sixth-grade class were behind the curtain on the stage in the Hollis Elementary School lunchroom. They were cleaning up what seemed like a couple of truckloads of trash left over from

1

their performance of *Planetary Peter Pan* the night before.

"We're moving right along," Bonnie commented. "We should be finished in another seven or eight years. Oh, there's another head over there. Why didn't we tell people to put their heads in the trash can when they were done with them?"

Unfortunately, no one had thought to tell the three kids who had played aliens in the sixth grade's updated version of *Peter Pan* not to toss their rubber and plastic alien heads on the floor backstage. In fact, no one had thought about the mess on the stage until the next day, when their teacher, Mrs. Doubleday, had told them they had to clean it up. "By lunchtime," she had said firmly.

So a few minutes before the lunch bell rang, they were still working frantically to get everything done. Tiffany Root, the class's biggest worrier, was looking doubtfully at a pirate's hat that someone had stepped on. "There's got to be *something* we can use this for!" she was saying. Louie and Larry Watson, identical twins known far and wide as the Human Demolition Team, were gleefully jumping up and down on one of the sets, reducing it to splinters. "I bet we can get it down to the size of a pack of cards," Louie was saying. And

Rocky Latizano, the class's most notorious eater, was standing in one corner scarfing down a candy bar. "I've got to keep my strength up," he mumbled when he saw Bonnie grinning at him.

"We don't need wastebaskets back here—we need *dumpsters*," grumbled Bob.

"Well, you wrote the play, Bob," Bonnie reminded him tartly. "If you were so worried about cleaning up, you shouldn't have written something with so many battle scenes. Besides, isn't it great to know that we don't have any more activities to worry about? The play is over, the cookie sale is over, the dance is over, the Night of a Thousand Pizzas is over. Really, with all that stuff behind us, plain old school is going to seem like a vacation."

Just as Bob opened his mouth to answer, a crackling noise erupted from the public-address speaker in their corner of the lunchroom.

"Students! Your attention, please!"

"Uh-oh," Bonnie muttered. "That's Mr. Haypence. I wonder what *he* wants."

Mr. Haypence was Hollis Elementary School's principal. Students in the school had learned to clench their teeth whenever they heard his voice on the P.A. system. It almost always meant something horrible was coming.

3

Once he had everybody's attention, Mr. Haypence cleared his throat richly for several seconds. Then he boomed, "Two weeks from today we will be welcoming Brookside Elementary School's volleyball team for Hollis's first annual volleyball tournament."

"Big whoop," said Bob sourly.

Obviously it was to Mr. Haypence. "This historic event will take place in the gym, and I urge all of you to honor us with your presence. I will be leading a special cheerleading section for any interested participants."

"*You'd* be great for that," Bonnie and Bob told each other simultaneously.

"Details will follow," Mr. Haypence continued. "For now, please return to your studies." Then he cleared his throat again—and in a creaky voice he yelled, *"Go, Hollis!"*

Bonnie groaned. "If he's going into cheerleading mode, I'm switching schools. I can just see him carrying pompoms and—"

Suddenly she noticed a little boy poking his head through the stage curtain. He was blond, freckle-faced, and skinny, with ears that stuck out, hair that stuck up in a cowlick, and a worried expression.

"Hi!" Bonnie said. "Are you looking for someone?"

The little boy jumped at the sound of her

voice. "Me? No," he piped. He pushed himself through the curtain and walked shyly toward her.

"What's your name? Do you go to school here?" asked Bob.

"Ryan. I'm in the second grade." Ryan turned and stared at Chantilly Lace, who was struggling toward the storage room with an armful of costumes. Tilly managed a feeble wave at them.

"We're cleaning up," Bonnie explained. "Want to give us a hand?"

"Well, not really," Ryan answered politely. "I'm just looking around. My teacher thinks I'm in the bathroom. I was just wondering if—" He broke off, looking worried again.

"If what?" Bob prompted him.

"Oh, nothing," answered Ryan vaguely. "Well, bye." He turned and pushed his way through the curtain again.

Bonnie smiled. "I guess we're a tourist attraction," she said.

"Are you almost done in here?" came another voice. Bonnie and Bob turned to see Ms. Weinstock, the school dietician, poking *her* head through the curtain.

Ms. Weinstock was small and thin, and had been perpetually nervous during her first few months on the job. Since she'd settled in, though, Bonnie thought she was much calmer—more like a real grownup.

She pushed her way through the curtain and clapped her hands. "Five more minutes, guys!" she called. "I want this stage spotless before the lunch bell rings!"

Rocky Latizano groaned. "Can't we finish *after* lunch?" he asked. "We're too weak from hunger to do a good job now!"

Ms. Weinstock grinned sadistically and left the stage.

Finally the lunch bell rang. Bonnie let out a sigh of relief.

Rocky hurled his way through the curtain and thudded onto the lunchroom floor. *"Let's eat!"* he shouted as he thundered over to the kitchen.

Bonnie glanced around the stage. "Looks clean enough to me," she said. "Well, let's go get some beef stew or whatever it is."

By the time she and Bob reached the lunch line, Rocky was already sitting down to lunch. As Bonnie watched, he ripped open one of his milk cartons and poured the contents down his throat. Then he grabbed a large spoon and dug into his bowl of stew.

"Arrwp!" he yelped after a second or two.

The buzz of conversation in the lunchroom

halted immediately, and everyone turned to look at Rocky's horrified face.

Rocky wiped his mouth, and with a jaunty smile yelled, "Pretty good, Ms. Weinstock. But don't you think the stew is a little heavy on the rubberbands?"

Bonnie picked a bowl of stew off the counter and stared at it.

"Rocky's right!" she said in astonishment. "Look!"

Poking through the gravy were dozens of tiny tan rubberbands.

Chapter Two
More Mysteries!

"Okay," said Mrs. Doubleday a few mornings later, "who's the big joker?"

Everyone in the class stared blankly at her. Homeroom bell had just rung, and all any of them had done was come into the classroom and sit down.

"I won't get mad if you'll just own up to it," Mrs. Doubleday went on.

More blank stares. Bonnie glanced around the room. Everyone else in the class looked just as confused as she felt.

"Fine." Mrs. Doubleday stalked to her coat closet. She yanked her coat off its peg, jammed her hand into one of the pockets, and pulled out a pile of bright-blue scraps. "There," she said, holding the handful of scraps out toward the class. "This is what I'm referring to."

"What is it?" asked Diego in a puzzled voice. "It just looks like some strips of cloth!"

"It's strips of cloth *now*," said Mrs. Doubleday. "But *yesterday* it was my silk scarf. And I don't appreciate it being hacked up like this."

By then Bonnie wasn't the only one staring around the room. *Who could have done such a crazy thing? Could it really have been someone in the class?* Bonnie wondered.

"Do you think someone's out to get you, Mrs. Doubleday?" asked Tiffany in a trembling voice.

With that, Mrs. Doubleday relaxed a little. "Well, someone's certainly out to get my scarf," she said with a faint smile. "I have to tell you, gang—this isn't very pleasant. For someone to wait until I was out of the room, and then to cut up something of mine like this—well, it gives me the creeps."

I agree that this is creepy, thought Bonnie. *But cutting up a scarf still doesn't seem like something one of us would do.*

"Well, I guess it's pointless to expect whoever did this to confess," Mrs. Doubleday said with a sigh. "Let's forget about it and get started with our morning. Trini, have you fed the fish yet?"

Trini Abella jumped to her feet. "I'm sorry,

Mrs. Doubleday. I totally forgot," she said quickly. "I'll do it right now."

At the beginning of the school year, the class aquarium had held a dozen goldfish. Then what Diego Lopez called "fish attrition" had set in, and now there were only two left—a black one with big, bulgy eyes, and an orange one with the stringiest excuse for a tail that Bonnie had ever seen.

Trini rushed over to the fishtank and began sprinkling fish food onto the water. Then she paused and stared into the tank. "What's the matter with the fish?" she asked in amazement. "Look at them!"

Everyone jumped up. "Hey, wait a minute, people!" Mrs. Doubleday protested. "Sit down and—" But it was too late. The whole class was crowding around the fishtank.

The week before, Tilly had brought in a little plastic castle for the bottom of the tank. "Bulgy and Carrot need a place to live," she had said with a half-embarrassed smile. "I feel sorry for them, swimming around and around without anything to hide inside when they get sick of us staring at them."

They were certainly hiding right then. The two of them were wedged into the castle so tightly that all Bonnie could see was their round, fishy mouths sticking out one side of the castle and the tips of their tails protruding from the other.

"They're stuck in there! They'll suffocate!" cried Tiffany.

"Don't be ridiculous. They're fish—they can't suffocate in the water," Jonathan Matterhorn said. "But they do look kind of strange."

"And it's not like fish to hide when there's food around," put in Diego. "When my fish at home see me take out their can of food, they practically jump out of the tank. Try tapping the castle with the net a little bit, Trini."

Trini gave the castle a gentle tap. The fish jerked and their tails quivered a little, but they didn't move.

"That's too rough!" protested Tiffany. "Fish are like all animals. You have to be gentle with them!"

She bent down and put her face right up to the tank. "Come on out, little guys," she said coaxingly. "No one will hurt you. We want to be your friends!"

Bonnie winced. Tiffany could overdo it sometimes. And it wasn't even working! At the sight of Tiffany's face looming in front of them, the fish had jammed themselves even tighter into the castle.

"Here, let me try!" said Louie Watson ea-

gerly. Before anyone could stop him, he had reached right into the tank and picked up the tiny castle. He pulled it out of the water and gave it a vigorous shake.

The fish plopped into the water.

"See?" said Louie. "You've just got to be firm with them, that's all."

But when he put the castle back into the tank, both fish darted toward it and crammed themselves into its tiny doorway. Once again, they wouldn't budge.

"They're scared," said Mrs. Doubleday slowly. "What on earth could be the matter? They were fine when I looked at them yesterday."

"The only time I ever saw my fish act like that was when my cat knocked off the tank cover and tried to catch them," Diego said thoughtfully. "But there's no cat here!"

Bonnie thought beef stew with rubberbands in it was sort of funny—once. But any joke can wear thin if it's repeated too often. In this case, once was too often. The main course they had the day after the scarf and fish episodes was called Luscious Pineapple Chicken. But the fact that each piece of chicken was studded with erasers made it seem a lot less luscious.

"What is going on here?" Jennifer Stevens

howled after her first bite. "Ms. Weinstock, are you trying to poison us?"

The whole lunchroom was buzzing with outrage. Everyone had given up on their chicken—except for Rocky. He was busily rolling chunks of it through his fingers to sift out the erasers. On one side of his tray, he put the erasers he found; on the other side, he piled up the cleaned-up chicken.

He picked up an eraser and shook it angrily at Ms. Weinstock as she approached. "Okay, very funny," he said with a frown. "Where's the real chicken? "

Ms. Weinstock pulled a chair up to the table and sat down. "Sorry, Rocky, that *is* the real chicken," she said. "Believe me, I'm just as puzzled as you are. I have no idea how this could have happened. Two days in a row!"

"Oh." Evidently Rocky's curiosity was now satisfied. "Well, who doesn't want their chicken?" he asked. "I'll take it. I've got a good cleaning system going here."

Bonnie shoved her plate across the table to him. Then she turned to Ms. Weinstock. "I don't understand why this is a surprise to *you*," she said. "Didn't any of the lunchroom staff notice the rubberbands or erasers while they were cooking?"

"Especially the rubberbands," Rocky put in.

"I mean, in chicken the erasers can pass for the tough parts. I think I even ate one or two before I noticed what they were."

Ms. Weinstock didn't bother paying any attention to *that*. Instead, she said, "Well, as you guys know, this is a state-of-the-art lunchroom. That's what Mr. Haypence wanted, and that's what he got. The whole oven system is controlled by a computer. There's even a computerized slicer to slice open the boxes of ingredients and a computerized can opener to open any cans we need. The contents of the boxes and cans get dumped into the mixing bowls and the empty containers move along a conveyor belt to the trash cans, while the food gets mixed up and sent on toward the ovens. It's really an amazing process."

"So something's wrong with the computer?" suggested Bonnie. "Maybe it opened the wrong stuff?"

Ms. Weinstock shook her head. "That's the part I *really* can't figure out. After the rubberband fiasco yesterday, we tested the system, and everything worked fine," she went on. "Besides, we don't *have* boxes of rubberbands or erasers in the cafeteria. We don't need office supplies in here! If the computer had been malfunctioning, it might have opened the wrong box of food—but how would it have gotten hold of a box of rubberbands?"

"I guess it's just sabotage, then!" said Jennifer angrily.

"I don't see how this could be sabotage," Ms. Weinstock said. "There's always someone in the kitchen in the mornings. No one could possibly sneak in without being caught."

"Then they did it the night before!" Jennifer said promptly.

"But we never cook the night before, so there wouldn't have been any stew to dump rubberbands into."

"Or chicken to mix erasers into," Rocky reminded her. "But actually this chicken isn't that bad." He pointed at the grubby pile of chicken bits on his tray. "See, I take these things here and mold them into kind of a drumstick shape, and—"

Ms. Weinstock jumped to her feet. "I'd better go check on how the other lunch tables are doing," she said hastily. Then she paused.

"It's probably just a weird coincidence," she said, rubbing her forehead wearily. "I'm sure it will never happen again."

"That's exactly the kind of thing a grownup would say," Bonnie scoffed to Bob later that afternoon. She was standing at Bob's locker waiting for him to get his books out so they could walk home together. "Don't you think it's weird that all these things are happening at once? The rubberbands, Mrs. Doubleday's scarf, the goldfish being scared, the erasers—how can all that be a coincidence?"

"If you can manage to find a connection between rubberbands and goldfish, Bon, you're a lot smarter than I am."

"Well, I can't help thinking someone's out to get *someone*," Bonnie persisted.

The two of them were passing the art room as Bonnie spoke. Outside the door was a little display window filled with lurching, bow-legged clay people. A poster in the window read, "How We Work and How We Play: A Ceramic Exhibit by Ms. Welmann's Second Grade."

Just as Bonnie finished her sentence, she and Bob heard a muffled crash behind them. They turned around quickly. "What's that?" Bonnie gasped.

A shadowy shape was just darting out of sight behind the display window. As Bonnie and Bob watched, one of the clay figures inside teetered wildly, then toppled over and smashed through the display window to the ground.

"It just missed us!" Bonnie gasped. "Do you think *that's* a coincidence?"

Bob looked a little shaken, but he nodded stubbornly. "Yup. I do."

But the next day convinced even Bob that something mysterious was going on.

Chapter Three

A Shredder Among Us?

"Ruined! My anteaters are *ruined!*"

The voice came echoing down the hall toward Bonnie and Bob as they walked into school the next morning. They took one look at each other and raced toward it.

"I think that's Mrs. Dowdy," panted Bonnie as she and Bob skidded around a corner.

Mrs. Dowdy was Hollis's home economics teacher. "Home economics is about *economy*," she always liked to say. "There's no reason to squander money on store-bought things when you can make them yourself for just pennies!" She was big on knitting one's own socks, making hairbands out of cut-up oatmeal cartons, and brightening up old clothes with glued-on felt flowers. (The kids who had to take her class were especially fond of *that* idea!)

Bonnie and Bob peered into the home economics room. The whole classroom was covered with tiny bits of green foam. Foam was scattered on the floor, on the desks, and on the rug Mrs. Dowdy had made out of pipe cleaners. In the center of the room, her skirt flecked with more bits of green foam, stood Mrs. Dowdy, wringing her hands.

Bonnie stopped in the doorway with Bob hovering behind her. "What's the matter, Mrs. Dowdy?" Bonnie asked. "Can we help with anything?"

"Bonnie! Bob! Look at this mess! Just *look* at it!" shrieked the home ec teacher.

"I see it," said Bonnie. "But what is it?"

"It's stuffing, that's what it is! Stuffing for the fifth grade's anteater project!"

"Oh," said Bonnie after a second.

Mrs. Dowdy grabbed an envelope off her desk, marched it over to Bonnie and Bob, and thrust it into their faces. "Look! This is the pattern we were going to use. It's so adorable— and now the whole project's ruined!" she moaned.

The words *Artie the Anteater* were printed in perky letters at the top. The picture showed a blobby-looking pink anteater with button eyes and tiny ants, made from beads, sewn onto its tongue.

I guess it's adorable, Bonnie thought, *if you like toy anteaters that look as though they came from the bottom of your great-aunt's workbasket.* "It's very nice," she told Mrs. Dowdy politely.

"Lovely," echoed Bob. Bonnie could tell by his tone of voice that he was trying not to laugh. Quickly she turned away to hide her own smile.

"We were going to make little Archie out of old washcloths. We wouldn't even have needed to spend good money on new fabric! We would have had seventy-eight little Archies, if the fifth graders had gotten to make them," mourned Mrs. Dowdy. "We were going to sell them in the hall outside the gym during the volleyball game and make *hundreds* of dollars. But I unlocked my door this morning and found all the bags of stuffing—fifty pounds of it—ripped open and scattered everywhere!"

This was starting to sound familiar. "You say the bags were fine when you left last night?" asked Bonnie.

"Of course they were! They were stacked neatly over by the window. I always tell my students to leave things neat and tidy, you know. Why, if you want to cultivate good work habits, it's the only—"

"I remember you telling us about that," said Bonnie quickly. "And the door was locked?" Mrs. Dowdy nodded vigorously. "But who would have done something like that?" mused Bonnie. "Who *could* have?"

"Probably some nasty students from another school," sniffed Mrs. Dowdy. "I bet they got hold of a master key and went around inflicting all *sorts* of damage."

"Was anything else in here wrecked?" asked Bob.

"Well, no," admitted Mrs. Dowdy. "Just the bags of stuffing. But that's enough, don't you think? Now we'll have to stuff all the little Archies with old rags! It's lucky I *have* so many rags on hand. Why, I never throw anything away. As I was telling one of my classes just the other day, I—"

"Oops! I think I hear the bell! Good luck with the Archies, Mrs. Dowdy!" said Bonnie. And she and Bob made their escape down the hall.

But it wasn't much of an escape. Bonnie could tell the minute she walked into homeroom that Mrs. Doubleday was in a terrible mood. Everyone was sitting extra-still at their desks, and Mrs. Doubleday was standing in the front of the room with menace in her eye.

"Thank you for honoring us with your presence, Bonnie and Bob," she said in a tight voice as the two of them walked into the room. "We were beginning to wonder if you'd decided to take a vacation today."

Uh-oh, thought Bonnie. *I can tell right away this isn't going to be a terrific day.* She glanced quickly at the clock. She and Bob were only a minute late, but it didn't seem like a good idea to argue. "Sorry, Mrs. Doubleday," she murmured as she and Bob hurried to their desks.

Mrs. Doubleday was usually pretty easygoing, but that morning everything seemed to be getting on her nerves.

"Can't you take your book out of your desk a little faster than that, Rocky?" she asked sarcastically when they were starting math.

"Jennifer, put that comb away," she said in the middle of social studies. "When I decide to turn my classroom into a beauty salon, I'll let you know."

"Sit up straight, Jonathan!" she scolded a few minutes later. "You're not watching TV, you know!"

"Oh, why do trucks always have to back up outside *our* window?" she complained a few minutes after that. "I can't stand that beeping noise!"

Except for a few isn't-she-being-horrible

looks at one another when Mrs. Doubleday turned her back, the class sat petrified. *There's no worse feeling than being stuck in a room with a teacher who's on the warpath,* Bonnie thought. *If it's someone you don't like, you can at least get mad. But if it's someone you do like, you keep worrying about what you've done to make them mad.* Bonnie could feel herself shrinking back farther and farther in her chair, hoping that Mrs. Doubleday wouldn't decide to start picking on her.

Unfortunately, it didn't work. "Bonnie, would you mind wiping that expression off your face?" Mrs. Doubleday suddenly asked.

"Wh-what expression, Mrs. Doubleday?" Bonnie faltered.

"You're looking at me as though I'm about to hit you!" snapped Mrs. Doubleday.

"Well, that's kind of what I'm thinking!" Bonnie blurted out.

"What?" the teacher asked in a shocked voice.

Bonnie clenched her fists inside her desk. *Be brave!* she told herself. *She's not going to kill you!* "Mrs. Doubleday, are you mad at us?" she asked. "Because if you are, I wish you'd tell us why! It's horrible not knowing what we've done wrong!"

There, she thought. *I don't care if she gets mad at me.*

But Mrs. Doubleday no longer seemed angry. She bit her lip for a second, then sighed and sat down at her desk. "I'm sorry, guys," she said, propping up her head with her hand. "I should have told you right away. My day got off to a very bad start. When I came in this morning, I found a whole pile of shredded paper on my desk. It was the book reports I'd stayed here late last night to grade."

"I didn't do it, I swear!" Tiffany burst out in a frightened voice.

"No, no, I know you didn't, Tiffany," said Mrs. Doubleday tiredly. "I don't think any of you did it. I shouldn't have taken my anger out on you anyway. I just wish I knew who *had* done it—and why."

"This is *really* getting mysterious," Bonnie murmured to herself.

"You know, something sort of like this happened to Mrs. Dowdy last night, too," said Bob. Quickly he described what he and Bonnie had seen in the home economics room. "I wonder if anything happened to any of the other teachers?" he finished.

"Hey, maybe it did!" Looking a little relieved, Mrs. Doubleday stood up. "I'll call the office and see if they've heard anything else," she said. "As long as I know someone's not out to get just me—"

She picked up the wall phone and punched in the office number. Then she paused, jiggled the receiver a little—and finally pulled it away from the wall.

Its severed cord dangled uselessly in mid-air.

"The phone cord has been cut!" Mrs. Doubleday said in amazement.

And that wasn't the only cord that had been cut. When Bonnie's class arrived at the gym that afternoon, Mr. Skinner announced, "Okay, buddies!" (He always called them buddies.) "Get those arm muscles limbered up! Today we're going to be doing a little rope climbing!"

"Oh, no," Jennifer said loudly. "My arms always get so sore when we climb ropes. It really stresses me out!"

"Jennifer, buddy, that's the point," said Mr. Skinner patiently. "See, if you do enough climbing, your arm muscles will become so strong that your arms won't get sore anymore!"

"But if I never do any climbing, they'll never get sore in the first place," muttered Jennifer as she got into line.

The rope was coiled around a special metal beam near the gym ceiling, and Mr. Skinner had to press a button to release it. When Mr. Skinner pressed it, the beam began to rotate slowly, and the rope started to uncoil.

"Okay, gang! Get ready for roping!" Mr. Skinner called jubilantly. "Here it comes! Down . . . down . . . down a little farther—hey, what's the matter?"

The matter was that there wasn't enough rope. Only half of it was there. That half was hanging limply in the air about fifteen feet off the ground—and it had been shredded into a frayed mass of fibers that looked more like a horse's tail than something anyone could climb. Clumps of fluff from the shredded end drifted gently to the floor.

"Whoa!" said Mr. Skinner. "What's going on here?"

Bonnie and the rest of the class squinted up at the ceiling, where the remainder of the rope was still coiled around the beam.

Mr. Skinner looked at the class with a puzzled expression. "It wasn't broken yesterday," he said. "The fourth graders used it. As a matter of fact, Billy Norton climbed all the way to the top and then got scared to come down, so I had to get a ladder and go after him. I saw the entire rope close up, and it was in really good condition."

"The end of the rope looks like someone's been sawing at it," Diego pointed out.

"Someone was *sawing* at it?" shrieked Tiffany. "I knew it! I knew it! There's some kind of maniac loose in school!"

"Oh, for pete's sake," said Diego in disgust. "I'm sorry I said anything."

"No! I know I'm right!" Tiffany's eyes were wide with terror. "It's the Shredder," she said in a quavering voice. "It's going through the school attacking things. First Mrs. Doubleday's scarf. Then the anteater stuffing. Then Mrs. Doubleday's papers and the phone cord. Then the rope. And I bet—I bet he's going to start in on *us* next!"

Chapter Four

A Lead at Last?

"*Tif*-fany ... *Tif*-faneee ..." moaned Bob in a ghostly voice at the lunch table the next day. "Does this salad remind you of anything?" He picked up a forkful and waved it back and forth in front of Tiffany's eyes as though he were trying to hypnotize her.

"What are you talking about?" asked Tiffany uneasily.

"The lettuce. It's ... it's kind of *shredded*, don't you think?" Bob gave a demonic cackle.

"Oh, shut up!" snapped Tiffany.

Bonnie could tell that Tiffany was having a rough day. All morning long the other kids in the class had been torturing her with comments about the Shredder. Finally Mrs. Doubleday had made them stop—but Mrs.

Doubleday wasn't sitting at the lunch table. Bonnie, Tiffany, and Jennifer were, along with Bob, Diego, Rocky, and Jonathan. With no teacher to keep them in line, the others were having a great time teasing Tiffany.

"Oh, don't make fun of Tiffany, Bob," Bonnie said. "It's not nice."

"No, go ahead! Make fun of me!" said Tiffany indignantly. "You're just afraid to admit there's something going on!"

"Oh, I admit there's something going on," said Bob cheerfully. He picked up a forkful of eggplant, looked at it for a second, and then put it back down. (The special lunch that day was something called Savory Eggplant Pie. It was grayish brown and tasted unbelievably bad.) "I just can't bring myself to believe that there's a Shredder out there, that's all. Why would some maniac want to pick on our school, anyway?"

"Haven't you seen any horror movies?" demanded Tiffany. "In movies, hatchet-wielding maniacs pick on kids all the time!" Most of the rest of the table was grinning at her, so she added sheepishly, "Not that I've seen a whole lot of slasher movies. They're so scary I usually have to keep my eyes closed during most of the film. I even get scared during *The Wizard of Oz*."

"Well, I've seen a bunch of those movies, too," said Jennifer. "And I think Tiffany's right. I mean, those weirdos in the movies attack kids just because they feel like it. It's the grossest!"

"I can't believe this!" Diego stopped pushing his eggplant around and put down his fork. "Those are *movies*, Jennifer. They don't prove anything! I think it's a bunch of kids, myself. Grownups wouldn't waste their time throwing foam around. And I don't see how one person could be doing all this."

"But why would kids put rubberbands in their own lunch?" asked Bonnie.

Diego nodded. "That's the only flaw in my theory. Maybe they're from another school, or—"

"Who doesn't want their eggplant?" Rocky broke in.

Everyone turned to stare at him.

"Well, it's not *that* bad!" he said defensively. "Why waste it?"

Six plates of Savory Eggplant Pie whizzed down the table toward him. "Thanks," Rocky said contentedly as he began digging in. "At least there aren't any office supplies in this."

That was true. The office supplies didn't come until later in the meal.

When it was time for dessert, Ms. Weinstock

started flashing the lights on and off. (That was the way she quieted down the lunchroom—or tried to. It never worked until she'd done it about fifty times.)

"People, I have some bad news for you," she called when enough kids had stopped talking for the rest of the room to be able to hear her. "There won't be any dessert today. We've—"

Rocky wouldn't let her finish. "You're trying to cheat us!" he bellowed.

"No, I'm not, Rocky," said Ms. Weinstock patiently. "It's just that—"

"I ate all that eggplant glop and now you're telling me I don't get the good stuff!" Rocky's face was purple with rage.

"Well, I'm sorry about it, Rocky, but when you hear—"

"You *want* us to be miserable, don't you?"

Ms. Weinstock actually stamped her foot. "Rocky, *listen!*" she shouted. "There are chunks of memo pad in the apple crisp!" A wave of giggles and a wave of groans simultaneously swept the lunchroom.

Rocky paused for a second, his mouth still open. "Well, we can work around that," he said much more quietly.

"Rocky, I'm not even going to consider letting you work around it," said Ms. Weinstock. "I'm just glad I asked the lunchroom workers to start checking the food before they serve it. I'm not going to let you eat pieces of paper and cardboard.

"I'm getting a little tired of all this food being ruined," she went on. "We've got a real mystery on our hands. And if any of you can solve it, I'll—well, I'll be so grateful I'll let you choose the lunch menus for an entire week."

"Hey, that's more like it!" said Rocky happily. "We haven't had pizza in a *long* time." Everyone else shuddered, remembering how the computerized oven had turned out a thousand pizzas instead of a hundred just a few weeks earlier.

Bonnie wasn't thinking about the lunch menu, though. She was thinking about solving the mystery.

I've always thought I'd make a great detective, she told herself excitedly. *This is my chance!*

She could just see the headlines in the newspaper: SIXTH GRADER BONNIE KIRK SOLVES MYSTERY THAT HAD BAFFLED THE EXPERTS. (Of course there weren't any experts at Hollis to *be* baffled, but that didn't matter.) YOUNGEST DETECTIVE IN CALIFORNIA HISTORY PITS SELF AGAINST THE SHREDDER AND WINS.

Oops! Bonnie thought. *I'd better keep the Shredder out of it. I know no such maniac ex-*

ists, but I don't like thinking about it anyway.
Bonnie pulled out her notebook and pen and
started making a list of the things a detective
would have to do first in a case like hers.

Well, first she'd start investigating the scene
of the crime, of course. And in this case, the
scene of the crime was...the lunchroom
kitchen!

Bonnie raised her hand. "Don't you think we
should check the rest of the food supplies?" she
asked when Ms. Weinstock nodded at her.
"Even if we don't solve the mystery, it would
be nice to know that none of us is going to eat
manila folders by mistake."

"That's an excellent idea, Bonnie," said Ms.
Weinstock. "Why don't you and a couple of
other people do that right now? Tiffany, you
go, and—"

"And me," said Rocky eagerly.

"Okay, Rocky," said Ms. Weinstock after a
second. "But don't you dare try any free sam-
ples while you're in there."

"Hey, I'm a detective, not a food snitcher!"
protested Rocky.

"Fine. Keep it that way. Bob, why don't you
go along, too? The boxes of food are in that
storage room off the kitchen."

"I hope you're convinced now, Bob," said Tiffany with a huff as the four of them walked toward the kitchen.

"Convinced of what? That the Shredder put the memo pads in the apple crisp? That's not exactly shredding, is it?"

He pushed open the storeroom door as he spoke, and they saw a shadow flit across the room.

"*It's in here!*" Tiffany screamed.

For a second Bonnie's heart stopped, but she gritted her teeth and peered around. "Oh, don't worry, Tiffany," Bonnie said with relief. "It's just a moth! See?" She pointed to a moth about an inch long that was swooping crazily around the lights.

"A moth is almost as bad as the Shredder," said Tiffany under her breath. For the rest of the time she was in the storeroom, she kept her eyes turned away from the ceiling.

All the boxes of food were lined up by category. "Egg noodles," Bonnie read aloud from one stack of boxes. "Chicken soup, canned carrots, bouillon cubes, tomato paste, enriched flour, baking chocolate, chocolate pudding, peanut butter, saltines, and dried figs." None of the cartons looked like they'd ever been touched, much less tampered with.

"Hmm. I guess we'd better pry them open and check, just to make sure," said Rocky. He strode toward the cartons in a purposeful manner. "We'll start with the pudding, I think."

"No, don't! We'll get into trouble!" Tiffany begged. She darted in front of Rocky as if she meant to throw herself on top of the cartons. As she did, she kicked the bottom carton of saltines out of its stack by mistake.

"Hey, look!" said Bonnie excitedly. "Those aren't saltines!"

The carton was exactly the same size as the others, but Tiffany read the label: "One thousand gummed bond envelopes. Yuck!"

"Yeah, the chili would be gluier than usual if those found their way into the pot," said Bonnie. "I guess we'd better go through all these boxes and see what else we can find."

The only other nonfood carton they found was filled with rubber gloves. Like the envelopes, it had been carefully concealed at the very bottom of a stack of same-sized cartons. But it was hard to imagine anyone thinking that kids wouldn't notice huge rubber gloves flapping around in their food.

I don't know what a detective would make of something like that, Bonnie said to herself. *This mystery is really getting strange now.*

"Your attention, please!" Mr. Haypence barked over the P.A. system.

Mrs. Doubleday looked up from the science textbook and checked her watch. "There's only half an hour left before the last bell rings," she said. "I hope this isn't important."

"Please report to the hallway outside the gym," Mr. Haypence continued as if he had heard Mrs. Doubleday. "It is *extremely* important—a matter of school security."

All up and down the halls, doors were opening and kids were streaming toward the gym. "Okay, we'll finish working on clouds tomorrow morning," said Mrs. Doubleday with a sigh.

But even Mrs. Doubleday looked a little startled at the sight that greeted them in front of the gym. The trophy case had been ransacked!

The trophy case was set into the wall just outside the gym door. It was filled with gleaming trophies that Hollis students had won over the years. (Well, half-filled. Hollis teams had never had that great a record.) Bonnie had always liked looking at them. There were trophies showing helmeted kids leaping into the air to catch footballs, and trophies showing kids swinging hockey sticks in a way that would have bashed their opponents' teeth out in real life. There were trophies of debaters in glasses standing at podiums and looking serious. There was even a trophy of a poodle posing proudly with its nose in the air, which had been won by a Hollis dog-grooming club that had met for a couple of years in the 1950s.

But that day the glass in the case was shattered. Shards of glass were lying all over the floor, and the trophies were toppled from their shelves. The poodle had fallen out of the case into the drinking fountain below. From where she was standing, Bonnie could see that its tail was bent at an awkward angle.

Mr. Haypence was standing grimly next to the trophy case, his arms folded. "Who is responsible for this outrage?" he asked sternly.

No one said anything.

"I want an answer!" bellowed Mr. Haypence.

Bonnie looked around. She couldn't believe a Hollis student would have done such a thing. Besides, she wondered, even if someone in the school had done it, did Mr. Haypence really think that he or she would confess in front of all those people?

"Never in the history of Hollis Elementary has there been such a shocking act of violence," said Mr. Haypence. His glasses were slipping down his nose, and he straightened them with an impatient gesture. "For the first time since I came to Hollis, I am embarrassed to be your leader."

"Oh, you're not our leader anyway," Bob whispered so quietly that only Bonnie heard.

Mr. Haypence was waving his arms like a conductor. "To attack our athletic department!" he boomed. "And to do it just before the first annual volleyball tournament! What will the Brookside students think of us? I can tell you. They'll think we're weaklings. . . ."

He had a lot more to say, but Bonnie didn't hear it. Something about the words "Brookside students" had set her mind working.

What was it Mrs. Dowdy said yesterday morning? Bonnie asked herself. *I can't remember her exact words, but it was something about students from other schools. . . .*

"Probably some nasty students from another school." That was it. Mrs. Dowdy had thought outsiders were the ones who'd scattered the green foam all over her classroom.

At the time Bonnie hadn't paid any attention. But as she stood in front of the smashed trophy case she suddenly wondered if Mrs. Dowdy could have been on to something. And Diego had said the same thing at lunch.

What if kids from the Brookside Elementary School volleyball team were trying to spook the kids at Hollis?

I don't have any real evidence, Bonnie mused. *But the Brookside kids do have a reason to have a grudge against us. And I really can't believe any of these tricks were played by a Hollis student.*

Well, it was the only lead she had. And a good detective should investigate all her leads, even if they did seem kind of far-fetched.

And I do want to investigate something, Bonnie said to herself. *I want to solve this mystery before anyone else gets a chance to do it!*

I hope Bob and everyone else are free tomorrow afternoon, she thought, *because I think it's time to take a little search party over to Brookside.*

Chapter Five

Vengeance at Brookside

"So anyway, I think it would be a good idea to check Brookside out," Bonnie finished.

Bob was staring incredulously at her. "And what do you think will happen when we get there, O world-famous detective? Will we catch the volleyball team tearing up anteater stuffing and have to make a citizens' arrest?"

Bonnie could feel herself blushing. "Well, I know we don't have much to go on," she began.

"Much? We don't have anything!"

"No, that's not true," Bonnie told him. "At least we know that the Brookside volleyball team has a motive, kind of." She turned to Diego. "You said you thought someone from outside might be doing this."

"And I still think so," said Diego. "That

doesn't mean I think it's the Brookside volleyball team, though. I just can't see any connection between a volleyball tournament and
Mrs. Doubleday's scarf getting shredded."

"Oh, come on!" Bonnie pleaded. "Doesn't
someone want to investigate *something?*"

Half an hour earlier, after finishing his
trophy-case speech, Mr. Haypence had told
everyone to go home. "I'm closing school early
today," he had said soberly. "I want all of you
to spend your extra free time thinking about
what's just happened."

Because school had been just about to close
anyway, there were only five minutes of "extra
free time" left, but Bonnie had used those five
minutes to round up a Brookside Elementary
School search party. The trouble was that she
seemed to be the only person who thought a
search party was a good idea.

Except, unexpectedly, Jennifer Stevens. "I
think you're right, Bonnie," she said. "We
should *definitely* check out the Brookside volleyball team."

"Hmm. Why do you think so, Jennifer?"
Diego asked. There was a wicked gleam in his
eye.

"Because there are probably lots of cute guys
on the team!" said Jennifer. Judging from her
expression, Bonnie thought, she must have

been wondering why he couldn't have figured that out for himself.

"That's what I thought your reason might be. Well, you've sure managed to sell *me* on the idea," said Diego with a grin. "Count me in, Bonnie!"

"I think Bonnie's right, too," Louie said. "I also think we should stop at one of those army-navy surplus stores on our way to Brookside and pick up a few hand grenades. We'll show those stupid Brookside kids not to mess with us!"

Bonnie laughed in spite of herself. "Do you really think a few rubberbands and a broken trophy case are worth an all-out war?" she asked.

"Well, sure!" said Louie. "We're supposed to have school spirit, aren't we?"

"*I* think it makes more sense to poison them," said Rocky grouchily. "After all, they're the ones who kept us from getting any dessert today. We could buy some bug spray or something, and hide under the tables in *their* lunchroom. When they brought their trays out we could—"

"Rocky, get serious! We don't even know whether they've done anything to us!" Tilly protested.

"That's right," said Tiffany. "I think the best

thing to do would be to forget all about this, Bonnie. We could get in an awful lot of trouble, you know. Let's just go home and do our homework."

"Tiff, you're such a chicken," Rocky grumbled in disgust.

"We won't get into any trouble just for looking around the school," Bonnie said quickly. "If all we do is peek in the windows, what are they going to do to us? We can pretend we've just moved here. And is there any reason why we *shouldn't* check out Brookside? No one has to come along who doesn't want to!"

"Oh, I guess I really want to come," Bob admitted. "I think it will be fun even if we don't find any clues. I was just giving you a hard time, Bon."

Except for Tiffany and Junior Smith, everyone else seemed to feel pretty much the way Bob did. And Junior said he'd go along anyway.

"Great!" Bonnie said. "Let's go investigate, then! The thing is, Brookside's pretty far away. We'll have to ride our bikes there. If I figure out the route, can everyone go tomorrow after school?"

"I think I have a doctor's appointment," Tiffany said nervously.

"Oh? Are you sick?" asked Bob.

Tiffany looked excruciatingly uncomfortable. She hated to lie, Bonnie knew, but she also hated to be left out of things. "Well, I . . . oh, that's right! I just remembered that my mother canceled it!" she said. "But I'm not riding in the street!"

That was why, the next afternoon, Tiffany was bumping laboriously along the sidewalk while the others sped through the streets toward Brookside Elementary. "Wait up, you guys!" she kept wailing from far behind them as she dodged toddlers on their tricycles.

Jennifer was biking in the street, but she wasn't very far ahead of Tiffany because she kept trying to steer her bike and brush her hair at the same time. Rocky was going slowly, too. That was because *he* was eating french fries as he pedaled along.

Bonnie was out front leading the rest of the pack. Behind her she could hear Louie chanting, "The Hollis Avengers! The Hollis Avengers! Get ready to meet the Hollis Avengers!" He and Larry kept ramming into each other. They had already fallen off twice each. It was lucky that the route to Brookside went through a quiet neighborhood with hardly any cars.

I hope they'll calm down when we reach the

school, Bonnie thought. *If they keep acting like that, we'll be really conspicuous.*

"Ka-boom! Charge!" Larry Watson yelled. He threw himself off his bike and raced toward Brookside Elementary School. "We'll show you!" he bellowed.

"Wait!" Bonnie shouted. "Louie, stop him!"

Louie was still on his bike. To stop his twin brother, he simply rode right into him. The two boys lay stunned on the ground for a second, but promptly bounced right back to their feet.

"We're not going to charge," Bonnie explained to Larry. "Remember? We're just looking around!"

Brookside Elementary was a long, low, modern building with huge windows. Behind it Bonnie could see a massive playground with a wooden castle at its center.

"It looks just like Hollis!" Tiffany said in surprise.

"What did you expect? Bars on the windows?" asked Bob.

"Well, I did think it would be more, uh, vicious-looking," confessed Tiffany. "Considering that the kids who go here are practically murderers, I mean. I guess they're good at disguising themselves." Bob shook his head wearily.

"So what's the plan?" Diego asked.

Now that they were actually there, Bonnie wasn't sure what the plan should be. The front of the school was deserted, but they couldn't keep hanging around there. It would attract too much attention. "I guess we should split up and look for clues," she said at last.

"I've got to look for a drinking fountain first," Rocky announced. "Those fries made me really thirsty. I'll check around back and see if I can—"

"Oh, no!" Tiffany suddenly hissed. "Someone's coming out of the school! Everyone look normal!" She gripped Bonnie's arm painfully hard.

It was true. A pleasant-looking woman was coming through the front door. She smiled at them as she walked past.

"I bet you're wondering why we're standing here," Tiffany blurted out.

The woman stopped and turned around.

"Well, actually, I wasn't," she said, "but now I am. I'm the principal here. Can I help you with something?"

"We're waiting for our parents to pick us up," Bonnie said quickly.

"We just moved here," Bob said at the exact same time.

The principal stared at them without saying anything. "Those aren't our bikes, either," Tiffany said nervously, pointing at the bikes. "That pink one right over there? It isn't mine."

"I see," said the principal in a bewildered voice.

Shut up, shut up! Bonnie was trying to send the message telepathically, but obviously Tiffany didn't have much ESP.

"Wow!" she said in a shrill voice. "I just realized that that pink one *is* mine!" And before anyone could think of a way to cover for her, she jumped onto her bike and veered frantically away.

Bonnie broke the silence. "I think she had somewhere to go," she said lamely.

"So it seems." The principal's voice was dry. "And I hope the rest of you do, too. Well, have a nice afternoon!" She walked briskly over to the parking lot.

Bonnie let out her breath in a big sigh of relief. "Let's split up right now," she said. "I don't want to go through that again—not that we're going to have to, without Tiffany here. Anyway, I'll take that wing over there by the playground."

"I'll come with you," Bob offered.

"And I'll go anywhere that I can find a drinking fountain," said Rocky in a weak, gaspy voice. "I'm *incredibly* thirsty now."

Quickly they agreed who would search where, and decided to meet again in fifteen minutes. Then they split up.

Bonnie and Bob were peering into what looked like a kindergarten classroom when they heard a hissing sound.

"Bonnie! Bob! Over here!"

Tiffany was crouching behind the corner of the building and peeking out at them. When she saw that they'd seen her, she came scrambling toward them. She was bent almost double, obviously trying not to be too visible. Bonnie stifled a giggle. Tiffany looked a lot like a chimpanzee in that posture.

"Is she gone?" she said fearfully. "I biked around the block and then snuck back around the other side of the school. Do you think anyone noticed me?"

"If they did, it was only because you were acting so stupid!" Bonnie exploded. "The principal wouldn't even have noticed us if you'd only kept quiet!"

Tiffany looked hurt. "Well, I was worried that she might think we were a street gang!" she explained in a meek voice.

"Sure," said Bob heartily. "A street gang

with pink bicycles. Well, here you are, anyway. Do *you* see any clues in there?"

Tiffany peered through the window of the kindergarten classroom. "Definitely! Look at those construction-paper sunflowers over on that wall—they're so *sinister!*"

Before Bonnie or Bob could answer, Rocky came rushing up to them. "Come over to the gym!" he panted. "I've just found the Brookside volleyball team. They're practicing!"

The gym was on the other side of the school. Unlike the rest of the building, it had only one window, a small, thick one. Jennifer was plastered over every square inch of it as she stared into the gym.

"Hey, let us see, too!" protested Rocky. He was practically dancing with impatience.

"In a minute," said Jennifer, without moving a muscle.

At last she turned away. "There's no one cute in there," she said disappointedly. "Hey, don't knock me down!"

No one was listening. Everybody was too busy trying to elbow someone else out of the way to get a better view.

Bonnie got one square inch of window down in a bottom corner. She stared eagerly inside, but all she could see was a bunch of torsos in Brookside T-shirts running back and forth.

"Boy, they look tough," said Diego. His square inch of window was up at the top. "No way is Hollis going to beat them."

"You're right," agreed Bob. "Look at that sneaky little guy in the middle there!"

Bonnie strained to see him herself. "You mean the one with the weaselly face?" she asked. "He looks like just the kind of guy who would put memo pads in apple crisp and knock over a whole caseful of trophies. Hey, maybe we should follow some of these kids home. You know, tail them! We might be able to find out—"

"What are you all doing?"

Bonnie and her friends whipped around in horror.

There, facing them with her hands on her hips, was the Brookside principal.

Chapter Six

Bonnie Kirk, School Sleuth

"Enjoying the game?" the principal asked dryly as everyone scrambled away from the window.

"I—I—we thought you had left!" stammered Bonnie. *What a stupid thing for me to say!* she thought furiously.

"I had to come back for something," said the principal. "Now, may I ask exactly what it is about volleyball practice that interests you so much?"

"Oh, it's not the volleyball!" said Bonnie with what she hoped was a merry chuckle. "We're just looking for a lost contact lens!"

"Really? Whose?"

"Mine," said Bonnie, Bob, and Diego at the same time.

"My, my," said the principal. "Isn't that an amazing coincidence! And have any of you found your lost lenses?"

"Well, no," said Bonnie. "But you know, I've been thinking. I can see pretty well without it anyway. How about you guys? Can you see okay?" Bob and Diego nodded eagerly. "Then let's just go home. I'm sure the lenses will turn up. Bye!" She gave the principal a cheery wave, and then she and her friends dashed around the side of the building to where their bikes were parked.

They fled the schoolyard as fast as they could. Tiffany was so startled she forgot all about riding on the sidewalk and rode in the street along with everyone else.

When they were safely away from the school, Rocky was the first to slow down. "We didn't really get enough time to look around!" he called to Bonnie. "Maybe we should go back tomorrow!"

"Forget it," Bonnie snapped. "We're *never* going back there again."

Even if someone from Brookside is guilty, Bonnie told herself angrily, *how did I expect to catch him or her by snooping around the school? The stuff that's been happening has been happening at Hollis, not Brookside! I wanted to be a detective so much that I got carried away.*

Bonnie was still upset over the Brookside episode the next morning, and she said so to Bob as they walked to school together. "I hate to admit it, but you were right," she finished. "It was totally pointless going over there."

"Oh, well, it's no big deal. We all had an adventure, anyway," said Bob generously. "You're not going to let it stop your investigation, are you?"

She brightened. "Well, no. As a matter of fact, I did have an idea last night, while I was lying awake kicking myself about how stupid I had been. If Mrs. Doubleday will let me, I'm going to visit all the homerooms in school to see if anyone else has noticed anything. That's *got* to turn up a lead or two."

Mrs. Doubleday said Bonnie's plan was okay as long as she made up any work she missed, so Bonnie decided to start with the kindergarten and work her way up.

The morning kindergarteners were pretending to be butterflies when Bonnie came in to talk to them. That meant that a few of them were flitting gracefully through the room, and the rest were making truck noises and stomping around as loudly as they could.

"Okay, kids!" called Ms. Strite, the kindergarten teacher. "Let's all stop being butterflies and sit down quietly in a circle. Bonnie wants to ask us some questions." She pointed at Bonnie, who was sitting on a stool nearby. Then she turned to a little boy who was writhing around on the ground. "Billy, when we stop being a butterfly we don't roll on people's feet," she told him. "We just quietly stop."

A little girl with one Snoopy barrette (fastened) and one Raggedy Ann barrette (unfastened) walked up to Bonnie and leaned on her knees. "I'm Tracy. Are you a babysitter?" she asked in a sniffly voice. She had a cold, and kept wiping her runny nose on the sleeve of her sweater.

"No, I'm not," said Bonnie, averting her eyes. "I'm just here to talk to you."

"Well, I'm going to ask Mommy if you can be my babysitter," Tracy announced. "I love you. *Ms. Strite*," she yelled, "*I just told Bonnie that I love her!*"

"That's fine, Tracy," said Ms. Strite calmly. "Now, let's give her a chance to talk to us. Okay, Bonnie," she said with a friendly smile. "See what you can do."

Bonnie pried Tracy off her knees and stood

up. The circle of kindergarteners stared sternly at her.

"Hi, guys!" she said. "I'm here today because I've been wondering if any of you have noticed anything strange going on in school recently."

"Like what?" the boy named Billy shouted out.

"Oh, something funny in your snacks," suggested Bonnie, "or maybe something that got wrecked when it wasn't supposed to be."

"Like what?" called Billy again.

"I'm not sure. Maybe an art project that got torn up, or—"

"I know something strange!" a boy in a bright green sweatsuit interrupted.

"What, Zachary?" asked Ms. Strite.

"No people live on Mars! That's strange!"

Bonnie tried not to smile. "It certainly is," she agreed gravely. "But I'm wondering about strange things that have happened in *school*."

"Oh! Oh! I know! I know something!" Tracy, the girl with the cold, was waving her hand so furiously that Bonnie was afraid she was going to tip over. "I know something strange that happened in school! Last week!"

"What, Tracy?" asked Bonnie.

"Someone tried to flush a cowboy boot down the toilet! Water came up all over the—"

"That's not quite what Bonnie means,

Tracy," said Ms. Strite. But Tracy's information had started the whole kindergarten snorting and gasping and shuddering with laughter.

"I think it's time for us all to turn into butterflies again!" called Ms. Strite decisively. To Bonnie, she said, "I'm sorry. I don't think you'll be able to get much out of them right now." Bonnie decided it was time to visit another classroom.

But in all of the classrooms she tried, Bonnie only found one kid who'd seen something strange. That was in Mr. Perez's fourth-grade class. Unfortunately, Mr. Perez wasn't in that day, and his student teacher, Ms. Rubin, was trying to run the class all by herself. She didn't quite know how to keep the kids in line.

"Now, Bonnie Kirk would like to—*shh!*—talk to us about—*shh!*—some strange things that have—*shh! shh!*—been happening in school. *Shh!*" Ms. Rubin said. "*Shh!* Bonnie, go ahead. *Shh!*"

Bonnie found that it was almost impossible to talk while Ms. Rubin kept making shushing sounds, even though it wasn't Bonnie she was trying to shush. "*Shh! Shh!*" Ms. Rubin said when Bonnie had finished. "Does anyone here have—*shh!*—anything to tell Bonnie? Yes, Claire?"

A shy-looking girl with blond hair stood up. "Well, last week I had to go into the locker room to get my extra pair of sneakers."

"*Shh!*" Ms. Rubin told the rest of the class. "No, Claire, not you. You go ahead. *Shh!*"

"Well, I was all alone in there, and I saw something very—"

"*Shh!*"

"—very scary. It was a sneaker."

"Oh, yeah, that's real scary!" a boy in the back of the room hooted sarcastically.

"*Shh!*" Ms. Rubin hissed at him.

"It *was* scary!" Claire insisted. "The sneaker was moving along all by itself!"

"Wait a minute," said Bonnie incredulously. "What do you mean, moving?"

"It was upside down, and it was kind of bumping along the floor."

"You're so dumb, Claire!" shouted the sarcastic boy at the back of the room. "Sneakers don't move by themselves." That time Ms. Rubin said "*Shh!*" so vigorously that her face turned pink.

"What did you do?" asked Bonnie. To herself, she wondered, *Do I believe this?*

"I ran out of there," Claire said simply. "I was too scared to watch any more."

Bonnie didn't know what to think. Claire looked like she was telling the truth—but how could she be? "Are you sure you didn't imagine it?" she asked.

"Of course not!" said Claire indignantly. "I heard the bumping sound before I turned around and saw the sneaker! You don't imagine a sound!"

I guess that's true, thought Bonnie. "Well, thank you very much," she said doubtfully. She turned to Ms. Rubin. "And thank you, too."

"Oh, it's no—*shh!*—trouble," said Ms. Rubin. "I was glad for the—*shh!*—distraction, to tell you the truth. *Kids! Please! Shh!*"

Bonnie walked tiredly toward her locker at the end of the day. She had spent all morning asking different classes if they'd noticed anything, and the only clue she'd turned up was almost too weird to believe.

I guess there's no point in going any further with this stupid mystery, she thought as she pulled her locker open. *I'm just wasting my—*

"Are you the girl who was in my class this morning?" came a whisper from behind her.

"Yes, I am." Bonnie turned and saw a freckle-faced little boy staring at her. He looked familiar, but she couldn't place him. Then she remembered. "You're in Ms. Welmann's class, aren't you?" she asked. "And wait—didn't I see you a few days ago, too?"

Bonnie hadn't been able to help noticing the boy when she was in the second-grade classroom earlier in the day. He had stared at her with such a guilty expression that she had been sure he had a secret he wasn't telling her.

"Ryan! That's your name, isn't it?" said Bonnie. "I remember you. You came backstage while we were cleaning up."

Ryan nodded miserably.

"Is there something the matter?" Bonnie asked him gently.

"You won't tell the police, will you?" asked Ryan.

Bonnie grinned. "I can't believe it's bad enough that I'd have to do that," she said. "You can trust me."

Ryan scuffed his sneaker along the ground for a few seconds before he answered.

"Well, you remember what you said about those saltines that were missing from the storeroom?" he muttered.

"Yes?" said Bonnie encouragingly.

"Well, uh, I know what happened to them." His voice had dropped to a whisper again.

"You do?"

"Uh-huh. I took them." Ryan's face was flaming. "I took them to give to my hamster."

The poor kid is really scared, Bonnie thought.

She bent down to him. "What's your hamster's name?" she asked.

"Slimer," he whispered.

Bonnie bit her lip to hold back a smile. "Well, Ryan, you won't do it again, will you?"

"No," said Ryan. "It's too scary."

"It's also wrong to take things that don't belong to you," Bonnie told him.

"I know," said Ryan. "I'll never do it again. You won't tell on me, will you?"

"I won't tell anyone about Slimer," she promised. "Thanks for telling me, though. And give Slimer a pat for me."

"I will." Suddenly Ryan looked a whole lot happier. "Bye!" he whooped happily, and raced away down the hall.

Bonnie checked her watch. *Maybe I'll do a little homework in the library before I go home,* she thought. *I might as well get* something *done today.* She grabbed the books she needed and headed down the hall toward the library. (Actually, the Hollis library was supposed to be called the Media Center, but no one except Mr. Haypence and Mr. Pratt, the librarian— a.k.a. the media specialist—called it that.)

When she walked into the library, Bonnie saw that Tiffany was there, too. She was sitting at one of the desks and scribbling furiously in a notebook. Stacks of books, encyclopedias, and magazines were piled high around her.

"Hi, Tiffany!" said Bonnie. "What are you working on?"

Tiffany turned around, and her eyes lit up. "Bonnie! I was just thinking about you!" she exclaimed. "I'm working on the mystery."

"The mystery? You're reading books about it?" asked Bonnie, bewildered.

"I'm not only reading about it. I've solved it!" said Tiffany proudly.

"You have? Tiffany, what's going on?"

Tiffany leaned closer.

"It's a *ghost*!" she whispered. "A ghost is attacking our school!"

Chapter Seven

Tiffany's Tactics

"Oh, Tiffany, give me a break!" Bonnie groaned. Mr. Pratt, the media specialist, shot her a warning glance.

"No, it's true! I can prove it!" whispered Tiffany, gesticulating wildly. "I've been doing a lot of reading. There's got to be a ghost in this school. Maybe lots of them! The kind of stuff that's happening at Hollis is what happens in houses that have a curse on them."

"What kind of stuff?" asked Bonnie.

"Okay, let me show you." Tiffany picked up an old book called *The Curse on Twelve Oaks Manor*. From the amount of dust on the binding, she was the only person in fifty years to have read it.

"This is a true story about this family who

had a curse on their house," she said. "It happened around the turn of the century. The family first figured it out when there was a mysterious rapping sound in the walls. See, that was the ghost knocking to signal them. Pictures kept falling off the walls, and then all their silver spoons got bent. It turned out there had been a murder in that very house a hundred years before."

She stopped and looked expectantly at Bonnie.

"I'm confused. What did the spoons have to do with it?" asked Bonnie.

"Oh, I don't know," said Tiffany irritably. "Maybe that was the only way the ghost could communicate. Anyway, all this shredding and rubberbands and scared goldfish stuff matches up exactly with what happens when a building is cursed. There must have been a murder on this very spot long ago! That's why there are so many ghosts hanging around."

"They're *not* hanging—" Bonnie started to say, but Tiffany didn't give her a chance to finish.

"Just look at this picture, Bonnie! It's a real photo of the family all this happened to. Don't they look terrified?"

Bonnie took the book and stared at the yellowed photograph Tiffany was pointing to. It showed an old-fashioned family sitting rigidly around their dining-room table. They didn't look especially terrified, even though there was so much food on the table that Bonnie thought they should have been afraid of eating themselves to death. She looked at the picture some more. To her, they just looked sort of glassy-eyed.

"So what happened to their ghost?" Bonnie asked. She handed the book back to Tiffany without saying anything about the picture.

"Well, they were just like you, Bonnie," said Tiffany solemnly. "They didn't believe it was a ghost. And one day, the house burned down!"

Again Tiffany seemed to be waiting for Bonnie's stunned reaction, but it never came. "The media center will close in two minutes," announced Mr. Pratt, cutting short Bonnie's education about ghosts.

"But our school's not going to burn down," whispered Tiffany as she gathered her belongings. "I'm going to take home every single one of these books and learn how to exorcise a ghost. That's the word for getting rid of ghosts," she explained importantly. "I'm going to lift this curse, Bonnie. And then goldfish will never have to be frightened in our school again."

"The media center is now closed," said Mr.

Pratt sternly. To show that he meant business, he clicked off all the lights.

"Oh, no! I haven't checked out any of my ghost books yet!" squeaked Tiffany in a panic. "Wait, Mr. Pratt! Wait!" Lugging a huge armful of books, she struggled over to the checkout desk.

I don't think I'll wait for her, Bonnie decided. *I doubt I can listen to any more of this stuff without cracking up.*

She waved goodbye to Tiffany and walked out into the hall. It was empty, and the lights were dim. Bonnie's footsteps echoed eerily as she headed toward the front door.

It's a little creepy when no one's here, she thought uneasily. *Tiffany's just being loony, but when I'm alone in an empty building, even I might start imagining things. . . .*

Suddenly a white, flickering shape shot straight down the hall about twenty feet ahead of Bonnie. Then, faster than Bonnie thought anything could move, it streaked out of sight around the corner.

Bonnie stood stock-still. Her blood was pounding in her ears.

She knew she wasn't imagining things. What she had just seen was real.

Or was it?

* * *

72

The next morning Bonnie and Bob walked to school together as usual, but neither of them was expecting the overpowering smell of garlic they encountered when they opened the front doors of the school.

"What's going on?" Bonnie sputtered. "Has there been another accident in the kitchen?"

"No," Bob choked back. "Look over there. It's coming from that locker!"

Bonnie looked where he was pointing and saw a locker door festooned with braids of garlic heads. They had been fastened on with big loops of masking tape.

"Hey, that's Tiffany's locker!" she said in surprise.

Then she realized what must be going on.

"I bet that's to keep the ghosts away," she told Bob, not sure whether she felt like laughing out loud or strangling Tiffany. Quickly she filled him in on their conversation in the media center the day before.

"So stinking up the school is supposed to lift this curse we're under?" Bob asked.

"That's right," came Tiffany's voice from behind them. "Garlic is a very powerful antidote against ghosts."

"It's powerful, all right," said Bonnie with a sigh.

"Oh, that smell isn't only coming from *my*

locker," Tiffany assured her. "I brought a lot more garlic with me this morning. I've been going up and down the halls pushing cloves of it through the vents in other lockers, too. I made sure to get them into both your lockers because you're friends of mine," she said proudly.

"Thank you, Tiffany," said Bob. "I feel more protected already."

He wasn't quite so polite at lunchtime, when Tiffany reached into a brown paper bag and dumped big handfuls of salt over everyone's food. "It was a medieval custom," she explained. "It's supposed to keep harmful spirits away."

Bonnie finally had to get firm with Tiffany the next day, when she found her out on the playground scaring the kindergarteners to death during recess.

Tiffany was leaning over the sandbox and lecturing a small bunch of wide-eyed children. "And they're *here!* Right here in our school!" she said somberly as Bonnie walked up next to her. "That's what happens when there's a curse on a building—ghosts come."

"Wh-what's a curse?" asked a little girl. Bonnie recognized her as Tracy, whom she had talked to two days earlier.

"A curse is a bad magic spell that gets placed

on a building when something terrible happens there, like a murder," Tiffany explained helpfully.

Tracy shrank back in alarm. "A m-m-murder?" she asked in a tiny voice.

"Tiffany!" scolded Bonnie. "Are you crazy? Stop scaring them! Don't listen to her," she told the children in the sandbox. "She's just trying to tell you a story."

"No, I'm not!" Tiffany protested in a wounded voice. "They saw the garlic on my locker, and I was just explaining why I put it there!"

Bonnie knelt down next to the sandbox and put on the most convincing smile she could. "Isn't she silly?" she asked the children. "She's doing all these things to make the story more interesting! But of course there's no such thing as a curse, and there's no such thing as ghosts."

And right at this minute, I wish there were no such thing as Tiffany Root, either, she thought, exasperated.

"Your attention, please! Your attention, please! This is a very important announcement!"

"Not again!" grumbled Mrs. Doubleday. She set her piece of chalk down with a snap.

Mr. Haypence's voice flowed into the air,

mellow and smooth, through the P.A. system.

"I hope all of you are aware that tomorrow is the day of our volleyball tournament with Brookside Elementary School."

As one, Bonnie's classmates turned to look at her. She stared fiercely at the top of her desk.

"Because time is short," continued Mr. Haypence, "I am officially declaring the school day over."

"*Yay!*" everyone shouted.

"Instead of finishing your studies, please proceed to the auditorium, where a pep rally is to be held."

"Oh, no," everyone groaned.

"I will personally teach you several Hollis cheers, and together we'll get that school spirit up, up, up! Teachers, please have the students in the auditorium by two-thirty."

It was 2:28. "I guess we'll have to re-postpone our talk about clouds," sighed Mrs. Doubleday. "Everyone line up, please, and no running in the halls."

But no one was really anxious to see Mr. Haypence perform Hollis cheers.

"Hurry! Hurry! Sixth graders, stop strag-gling!" he boomed from the podium as people began filing into the auditorium. "There's no time to waste! Some of these cheers are quite complex!"

"Is this going to be as horrible as I think it will be?" Bonnie whispered to Bob as she headed toward the end of a row of seats. "Because I—*ouch!*" she yelped.

She had just plunked herself down into her seat, but something very sharp had somehow gotten there before her.

The auditorium fell silent for a second. Everyone had heard her. Bonnie would have been embarrassed if she hadn't been so mad.

She jumped to her feet. The end of a spring was poking right through the vinyl seat covering. It was as pointy as a pin, and much bigger.

As Bonnie looked more closely, she realized that the entire seat had been torn to bits. *No wonder a spring is poking out,* she fumed. *This chair looks like a rat's nest inside!*

"Can we assist you with anything, Bonnie?" asked Mr. Haypence acidly.

"Well, as a matter of fact you can," Bonnie answered just as sharply. "You can give me a new chair. This one's been totally torn apart."

"What do you mean? Let me see," said Mr. Haypence. He clumped down the steps toward her.

"Hmm. You're right," he muttered when

he'd studied the seat. "There must have been a design flaw somewhere. These are supposed to be the top of the line! Well, that's a pity, Bonnie. But you'll be standing up to learn the cheers anyway."

As Mr. Haypence strode back up to the podium, Bonnie turned to Bob.

"Some design flaw," she said angrily. "This chair's not worn out. It's been torn up by whoever else is causing all the trouble in this school. Well, I've had it.

"I've *had* it with this ghost or maniac or Shredder or whatever it is. I'm not sitting on any more wires or eating any more rubberbands or smelling any more garlic. I'm going to track it down tomorrow. And *everyone's* going to help me!"

Chapter Eight
Trapped!

It was the day after Mr. Haypence's pep
rally, and the volleyball game was due to start
in a few minutes. School had just let out, and
Bonnie and her friends were full of high spirits—not volleyball-game high spirits, but
mystery-solving high spirits. They had agreed
to meet in the lunchroom, and were going over
strategy.

In the case of the Watson twins, "strategy"
meant bashing the mysterious culprit over
the head when they caught him or her (or it).
Toward that end, each twin was armed with
a hockey stick. Diego, the science whiz, had
brought a periscope he'd made at home. "For
seeing around corners," he explained. Rocky
had brought a pair of handcuffs his aunt, who

was a police officer, had given him for his birthday. Junior Smith hadn't brought anything special, but he planned to give the culprit one of his business cards if he caught him. "Just in case he needs a lawyer," he explained. "Not that I'm a lawyer, but maybe he won't be too choosy."

And Tiffany was wearing an enormous necklace made of braided garlic heads. (Mrs. Doubleday had finally made her strip the garlic off her locker, but Tiffany had saved it.) In addition, she was carrying a wooden spoon.

"What's that for?" Bonnie asked.

"Well, if you meet a vampire you're supposed to drive a wooden stake through its heart," Tiffany told her. "I figured it might work for a ghost, too. But we didn't have a wooden stake at home."

"Glad you're so well prepared," Bonnie said dryly. *I can't quite see Tiffany driving a wooden stake or even a wooden spoon through anyone's heart,* she thought. *But if it makes her feel better...*

"Okay, guys," Bonnie went on. "We'll split up, and each person will take a different section of the school. Do you all know where you're supposed to go?"

Everyone nodded. "Good," said Bonnie. "Now, don't turn on any lights, and remember not to make a lot of noise! If we're going to catch this person in the act, we can't let on that we're after him or her. It's lucky the volleyball game will be going on at the same time. All the noise from the gym will cover our tracks."

"Here come the Brookside buses now," announced Tilly. She was looking out the lunchroom window. "The team's getting off."

I hope the principal didn't come along too, Bonnie wished. *I'd hate to run into her again.*

Suddenly she noticed that Tiffany was biting her nails and looking even more nervous than usual. "What's the matter, Tiff?" asked Bonnie.

"Well, don't you think we ought to go to the game?" Tiffany said. "I mean, Mr. Haypence wants us to be showing school spirit and everything! Maybe we should start our search tomorrow."

First she's worried about vampires, and now she's worried about school spirit! Bonnie thought in exasperation. "Tiffany," she said patiently, "don't you think we're really showing more school spirit by solving this mystery? Look how glad everyone in school will be when they're not getting poked by springs and choking on erasers! Believe me, the volleyball game doesn't need us. The mystery does."

"Well, okay," said Tiffany doubtfully. "But I wish we could ask Mr. Haypence's permission first."

"That would *not* be a good idea," said Bob instantly. "He'd only try to rope us into learning more cheers."

Everyone shuddered, including Tiffany. Mr. Haypence had gotten a little over-involved with his cheers during the pep rally. He had jumped up and down and screamed, and his glasses had gotten all fogged up. It had been embarrassing to watch him make a fool of himself.

"The rest of the Brookside kids are coming into the school now," said Tilly.

"Okay," Bonnie said. "Let's wait five more minutes, until everyone's in the gym. Then we'll start hunting."

"Five minutes? Good," said Rocky. He stood up and pulled a squashed-looking, napkin-wrapped package out of his back pocket. He unfolded the napkin and revealed a cold, battered cheeseburger. "That will give me time to have a little snack. Anyone want a bite? No? You guys are crazy."

Once again Bonnie was prowling through a dim hallway, and once again she couldn't help feeling that something mysterious was lurking in the shadows. She was checking out the rooms in the farthest wing of the building, and she kept wishing she'd chosen to check the rooms closest to the nice, lighted, noisy gym instead.

Whenever she turned around, weird shapes seemed to dart into corners. Wherever she walked, hidden whisperers seemed to grow suddenly quiet. Was that a hatchet hanging over the art room door? (No, it was a canoe some kid had made out of toothpicks and felt.) Had the door to the stairs been open before, or had someone just slipped through it and left it ajar? And what was that dark, ominous stain on the window at the end of the hall? Could it be blood?

No, it couldn't. Bonnie tiptoed over to the window and saw that the "stain" was just a sticker shaped like a football helmet.

Why would there be blood on a window, anyway? I've got to calm down, she told herself. *A good detective doesn't get flustered so easily.*

Then she really did hear her name. "Bonnie! Look at this!" Bob's voice called in a hushed voice.

He was running down the hall toward her on tiptoe. "I've got another clue," he panted. "It was in the music room. The door was un-

83

locked. I think Ms. Manzanella's at the volleyball game."

He held out a spiral notebook—or what had once been a spiral notebook. What Bonnie saw was mostly just the spiral wire part, with a few tatters of paper attached.

"The whole room is covered with scraps of paper," Bob said. "And someone's been attacking the curtains, too. They're all ripped and stuff. So maybe our suspect is lurking around there somewhere! Want to come and see?"

That sounds particularly uninviting, Bonnie thought with a shudder. *Do I want to go see a place where a maniac might be lurking? Well, I guess real detectives don't let themselves stop to think about things like that.*

"Of course I do!" she said out loud. "Let's go!"

The two of them started tiptoeing toward the music room. But after a few seconds, Bob suddenly stopped.

"What is it?" whispered Bonnie.

"I think someone's following us," he whispered back. "I heard footsteps."

Bonnie and Bob froze in their tracks—and so did whatever Bob had heard. "I don't hear anything," said Bonnie through chattering teeth. "L-let's keep going."

But after a few more steps, she heard the

sound, too. It was a hushed, brushing noise, as though whoever was following them was wearing socks but no shoes.

Bonnie whipped around in her tracks. "Who's there?" she called bravely down the shadowy hall.

There was no answer.

"It's probably the janitor cleaning the halls or something," Bonnie said. "Let's stop thinking about it."

They couldn't quite manage that, but they did get to the music room faster than they ever had before.

"See what I mean?" murmured Bob.

Bonnie did. At the windows the curtains hung torn and jagged, and a blizzard of paper had been tossed all over the floor.

"At least it's pretty small-time stuff," she said in a low voice, trying to keep her courage up. "So far we've been—wait a second!" She squinted into the gloom. "Look!" she said, pointing at the drum set off in the corner. "There's a big hole in that drum over there!"

Bonnie and Bob tiptoed into the dark room to look at the drums. It was true. The biggest drum had been ripped open.

Bonnie shivered. "This is so creepy!" she whispered. Then something caught her eye, and she peered into the hole in the drum.

"Hey, Bob! Look in here—there's a lot of shredded cloth and rope fibers and shredded paper. There's even a piece of Mrs. Doubleday's scarf." She began to poke around inside the drum some more.

"Hello?" someone asked in a trembling little voice.

Bonnie jumped a mile into the air and screamed at the top of her lungs.

"No, no!" A tiny form quivered at the door of the music room, and began to cry.

"It's just a kid!" said Bob swiftly.

Out in the hall, Bonnie heard Rocky yelling, "Hey, I think someone's in trouble! It's coming from around the corner! This way!" Then she heard footsteps skidding down the hall toward the music room. In a second, Rocky was at the door. He reached in and switched on the light. Behind him, Bonnie could see Diego, Tiffany, and the rest of her friends, all looking pale and frightened.

In front of them, cowering over by the piano, was Ryan, the second grader who had told Bonnie about his hamster three days before.

"What's that kid doing in here?" thundered Rocky. "What's going on?"

"Don't sound so mean!" Ryan began to cry harder. "I—I just want to talk to *her!*" He pointed at Bonnie. "I've been following you and following you, but I was t-too scared to say anything!"

Quickly Bonnie crossed the room to him. "Why were you looking for me, Ryan?" she asked.

Tears gushed out of his eyes. "Because—because you've got to help me! Slimer is lost!"

"*Slimer?* What're you talking about?" Rocky asked, completely puzzled.

Bonnie motioned for him to be quiet. "Slimer the hamster?" she asked Ryan.

He sniffed. "Uh-huh."

"It's lost here in school?"

"Uh-huh. I went down to look for him in his box, and he wasn't there! Please, you've got to help me find him!"

"We don't have time for that," Rocky began impatiently. But once again Bonnie shushed him.

"I guess I didn't understand about Slimer," she said to Ryan. "I thought it lived at your house."

"No, he lives here," said Ryan. "But no one knows that! Slimer's my *secret* hamster!"

"And where's its box?"

"Well, right now it's down in the furnace room," Ryan told her.

Bonnie's heart sank. Finding a hamster that had gotten lost in a classroom was one thing.

Finding a hamster that had gotten lost down in the basement was another.

"Well, Ryan, I'll give you a hand," she said. "But I'm not sure we're going to find Slimer. My friends and I have been looking all over the school for—for someone else, and we haven't seen any signs of a hamster so far. That's right, isn't it?" she asked her friends. They all nodded.

"We'll give it a try, though," said Bonnie encouragingly. "Why don't you take me down to Slimer's box, and we'll start looking there?"

"What about the rest of us?" asked Diego. "Want us to keep on looking for *our* Slimer?"

"I guess you might as well," said Bonnie. "Let's all meet back here in half an hour and then decide what to do."

Half an hour later a dejected-looking group reassembled in front of the music room. Bonnie and Ryan hadn't found Slimer, and the rest of the kids hadn't found the mysterious culprit.

"I don't know why I should feel bad about it," said Tiffany dolefully. "I mean, it's not as though I wanted to come face to face with a ghost! But I hate to give up without having found out anything."

"We didn't have any luck either," said Bonnie.

"Well, we didn't try the gym," Ryan said hopefully. "We could go there."

"Oh, no," said all the sixth graders instantly.

"Why not?" asked Ryan.

"Well, because there's a volleyball game going on," Bonnie began, "and we don't want to have to cheer at it—"

She broke off abruptly. That didn't sound like a very good reason for not looking in the gym. "Besides, there are so many people there that we wouldn't really be able to look very well," she corrected herself.

"Well, they could help us look!" said Ryan. "Please, Bonnie! I know Slimer's scared without me!"

"But I—" Then Bonnie stopped again. *I'm being awful,* she thought. "Oh, okay," she said. "Let's go look in the gym."

"I'll help, too," Bob offered.

"Hey, so will I," said Diego. "I'd rather look for a hamster than just go home."

It ended up with everyone deciding to go look for Slimer in the gym. "After all, we really should show some school spirit," Tiffany said.

"Besides, I want to get another look at the boys on that volleyball team," said Jennifer.

"And *I* want to see what Mr. Haypence looks like with his cheering squad," Jonathan said. "So let's go for it!"

It wasn't much of a cheering squad: just Mr. Haypence and three fourth graders, and the fourth graders were sitting exhausted on the floor when Bonnie and her friends slipped into the gym.

Mr. Haypence was carrying a megaphone. He was also wearing the terrible combination of a royal blue sweatsuit and his regular brown oxfords. "Go, Hollis!" he bellowed. "G-O spells *go!* N-O spells *no!* Hollis, you will *go-go-go!* Brookside, you will *no-no-no!*"

"The man's a genius," said Diego with a grin. "Can you believe he actually wrote that himself?"

Ryan was starting to fidget. "Can we look for Slimer now?" he asked.

"Sure," said Bonnie. She turned to her friends. "Why don't you guys sit down and watch the game? I don't think we all need to go crawling around the bleachers."

It was bad enough with just two of them doing it. The stands were pretty full, and Bonnie couldn't help bashing into people's ankles as she wriggled in and out of the bleachers. "Excuse me, excuse me," she kept saying. "I'm just looking for something."

"Sorry," she told a woman as she surfaced next to her. "I'm just looking for something."

"A lost contact lens?" came a dry voice.

Bonnie glanced up in shock. The woman she'd come up next to was the Brookside principal!

"Uh, yes," Bonnie managed to say. "Well, see you!" Horrified, she dove back down again, clambered to the ground, and ran behind the bleachers to the far end of the gym.

That was how she found the wrestling mats that had been stored behind the bleachers. They were neatly stacked next to some barbells. Neatly, except for the fact that they'd been completely shredded in the middle. And sleeping in the middle of the shreds was... what?

It was some kind of animal. It was cream-colored, and it looked like a weasel or a mink. It was about two feet long, and it was sleeping curled up.

Bonnie must have made a sound, because the creature opened its eyes. It blinked up at her sleepily. Then, like lightning, it jumped up onto the bleachers and raced away.

Before Bonnie could follow it, she heard a piercing scream.

"Help! Help! It's on my lap! Get it away!"

Then there were so many screams that they completely drowned out the noise of the volleyball game.

Bonnie scrambled up onto the bleachers again to see what was going on.

The creature was racing madly back and forth across the laps of an entire row of people. The volleyball players had frozen on the court to watch it. Mr. Haypence had stopped in mid-cheer. And about forty people on both sides of the gym were screeching their heads off.

"*Mad dog!*" shouted one man. "It has rabies! It's foaming at the mouth!"

"I'm suing!" shouted Junior.

"I'm allergic to mad dogs!" wailed Tiffany.

"If you'll all be quiet, we can resume the game!" Mr. Haypence bellowed.

Then still another sound rose above the screams. It was the happy shout of a little boy.

"*Slimer!*" yelled Ryan. He dashed into the middle of the volleyball game and scooped up the animal, which had finally left the bleachers. "I've found you. Bonnie, this is my hamster!"

Chapter Nine
Meet the Criminal!

"*Hamster?*" said Bonnie incredulously. "That's no hamster, Ryan! That's our Shredder!"

At exactly the same time, a boy on the Brookside volleyball team called out, "Hey, Dad! There's our ferret!"

"It's not a ferret!" yelled Ryan. "It's my hamster!"

Now a plump, dark-haired man on the Brookside side of the gym stood up. "No, it's a ferret!" he yelled back. "I should know! It's from my pet store!"

In the meantime, the ferret, excited by all the hubbub, had wriggled out of Ryan's arms and leaped into the other side of the stands.

"Whatever it is, it's digging around in *my*

raincoat!" the Brookfield principal called out in an amused voice. "Would whoever owns it please come and get it?"

The dark-haired man in the stands began making his way toward her, but it seemed that the ferret had other ideas. It hurled itself off the woman's raincoat and streaked down onto the floor again. Startled, the volleyball players lunged out of its way.

"Oh, catch him!" Ryan pleaded shrilly. "I *know* Slimer misses me!"

It didn't look that way to Bonnie, but she didn't tell Ryan that. She rushed over to the Brookside principal. "Toss me your coat!" she called.

Without a word the principal balled up her coat and tossed it down. "Thanks!" called Bonnie.

Then she turned to her principal. "Mr. Haypence! It's right behind you! Here, catch!" she yelled. And she hurled the balled-up raincoat straight at Mr. Haypence's chest.

He's going to miss, she thought.

But Mr. Haypence didn't miss. He caught the raincoat. He spun around. He dropped the coat nimbly onto the ferret. And he scooped up coat and ferret into one wriggling package.

"There," he said, panting slightly. "Now will someone have the goodness to relieve me of this creature? And after that, will someone kindly inform me what is going on?"

The Brookside volleyball player who'd called to his father came running up. He grabbed the coat-covered ferret gingerly. "What do you want me to do with it, Dad?" he called up to the man in the stands.

"Just hold it!" called his father. "I'm coming down!"

"Dad, it's wriggling all over the place! I don't think I can hold onto it!" the boy protested.

"Don't you dare drop it!" his father ordered. "I'm not going to lose it a second time!"

"But he's my hamster!" Ryan wailed forlornly.

"No, I'm afraid it really is my ferret," said the dark-haired man kindly. He took the struggling bundle of ferret from his son. "Now, I'm going to go put it in my car where it won't be able to get away. And then I'll come right back and explain all this."

"That would be a most welcome change," said Mr. Haypence. He straightened his glasses and smoothed his hair. "I have the feeling no one around here has been telling me what's been going on." He eyed Bonnie and Ryan sternly.

Then Mr. Haypence seemed to remember that about two hundred pairs of eyes were on him. "There will be a fifteen-minute break," he called to everyone in the gym. "Players, why don't you go back to the locker room and rest up? And spectators, please help yourselves to the delicious punch in the hall. It was made by members of the P.T.A. from all-natural ingredients, and I feel sure you'll find it refreshing."

At first no one seemed to want to go. Bonnie could hardly blame them. What was happening in here had to be more interesting than a cup of all-natural P.T.A. punch. But Mr. Haypence glared around so fiercely that most of them stood up reluctantly and began filing out into the hall. At last the only people left in the gym were Bonnie, Bob, Mr. Haypence, Ryan, the pet store owner's son, and the Brookside principal, who was listening quietly in the stands.

I guess she has a right to be here, Bonnie thought. *After all, we did capture it with her coat.*

As the gym emptied, Mr. Haypence turned to Bonnie and Bob. "And now, you two, suppose you tell me exactly what part you played in that little scene," he said.

"Mr. Haypence, I promise I will," said Bonnie. "But before we do that, could we talk to Ryan?" She pointed at Ryan, who was hunched miserably on the floor by the bleachers. "I think he's really upset. And please, Mr. Haypence, don't be too mad at him. I know he didn't mean to cause any trouble."

Mr. Haypence didn't answer that. "Ryan!" he called sternly. "Come over here, young man!"

Ryan wiped his eyes on his arm and walked draggingly over to them. "Are—are you going to call my parents?" he asked.

"We'll see about that later," said Mr. Haypence. "For now, I'd like to hear exactly what you know about that animal."

"He's my hamster!" said Ryan despairingly, for about the fourth time. "I bought him with my own birthday money! Only Mommy and Daddy won't let me have a hamster. So I decided to keep him here at school. I thought that if I kept him here, no one would ever find him!"

"Why didn't you buy a cage for it?" asked Bonnie.

"I didn't have enough money left," explained Ryan, "so I thought I'd just use an old box. I moved the box around every night so that no one could find it. And Slimer was always sleeping in the box when I came to feed him in the morning. But this afternoon when I decided to check on him, he was gone!"

"I have a feeling it's been gone lots of times,"

said Bonnie. "If it could shred up those big leather wrestling mats, it was probably easy for it to tear up Mrs. Doubleday's scarf and open Mrs. Dowdy's bags of stuffing. It must also have been responsible for scaring the fish in our classroom, biting through the rope in the gym, and even making that sneaker move!"

Bob nodded slowly. "It must have been looking for lots of soft things to build a nest to sleep in. Remember all the shreds we found in the drum?"

"And if Ryan had been moving the box around every night, that explains why Slimer was able to attack so many different parts of the school," Bonnie said thoughtfully. "I bet it knocked over the trophies and the ceramics as it was running around."

Mr. Haypence looked totally puzzled. "You mean this—this *animal* has been behind all the strange things that have been happening at Hollis?" Bob and Bonnie nodded.

"I'm sorry," Ryan sniffled. "I didn't know a hamster could do stuff like that!"

"A hamster couldn't," came a voice from behind Mr. Haypence. The pet-store owner had come back inside. "But a ferret could, especially a young one. And this one is very young."

"But when I bought him, the boy who sold

100

him to me said he was a hamster!" Ryan protested.

The pet-store owner shook his head ruefully. "That's the part that needs explaining," he said. He put an arm around his son. "Tony—that's this character here—was watching the store for me while I went out to do a couple of errands. My name's Rob Vilas, by the way. Anyway, it was late on a Friday afternoon, and I didn't think we'd have any more customers.

"Now this is where it gets complicated. We'd gotten a new shipment of baby ferrets that morning, and I didn't have any place to put them except in one of our big hamster cages. But I forgot to take the sign off the cage and put up a new one saying they were ferrets."

Tony's face was crimson. "So in comes Ryan," he chimed in, "and I was—well, I was kind of reading a comic book. He pointed at the hamster cage and said he wanted one of those. I asked him if he wanted any help picking it out—"

"And I said no," Ryan went on. "I said I could pick it out myself. And I did. I didn't *think* it looked too much like my friend Billy's hamster, but then I just decided, oh, well, there must be lots of different kinds. So I put it in the box I'd brought with me, and I closed up the box, because I didn't want my mother to see what was inside. So I took the box home and put it in the garage overnight. Then I took it to school early on Monday."

"The part I feel the worst about," said Tony, "is that ferrets sometimes bite. You could have ended up needing stitches, Ryan!" He turned to Bonnie, Bob, and Mr. Haypence. "I was planning to put the hamster in the box for him. But when he came up with it already in the closed box, I assumed it really was a hamster, and so I just went ahead and rang up the sale."

"So Ryan went off home," said Mr. Vilas, "and I came back. Needless to say, I was not thrilled to find that Tony had sold one of my hundred-dollar ferrets for five dollars. But what could I do? The ferret was gone, and I never expected to see it again."

"I never expected to see it in the first place," boomed Mr. Haypence. Ryan looked up at him fearfully. "Would you say a ferret is a destructive animal?" Mr. Haypence asked Mr. Vilas.

"Well, not if it's kept properly," Mr. Vilas said carefully. "The young ones do need plenty of exercise, of course, and you have to watch them to make sure they don't tear things up. They mostly sleep during the day and wake up toward the end of the afternoon, so the time you really want them caged is at night."

"And most of these mysterious things happened at night!" Bonnie filled in. "But that still doesn't explain all the weird stuff that happened in the lunchroom," she continued. "All those rubberbands, and the erasers—how could that have anything to do with Slimer?"

She turned to Ryan. "I know you said you took a box of crackers to feed your hamster, but—"

"I have to tell you something," Ryan interrupted urgently. "But I can't say it in front of these guys."

Bonnie bent her head down, and Ryan whispered, "I—um—I kind of took a few other boxes of stuff, too. I didn't want anyone to know what had happened, so I just filled in the spaces with some other boxes that were the same size—I found them in one of the supply closets down in the basement. I guess the computer opened the wrong boxes by mistake." He fell silent for a moment, and then he asked in a quavering voice, "Do you think I'll have to go to jail?"

What Ryan called "whispering" wasn't exactly quiet, though, and anyone within ten feet had heard what he said perfectly well. So it wasn't really surprising when Mr. Vilas joined in the conversation.

"Oh, you won't have to go to jail on account of me, Ryan," he said quickly. "After all, you were just feeding my ferret for me." He took out his wallet. "I'd be happy to pay for whatever food was used while the ferret was in Ryan's care," he told Mr. Haypence. "And I'll refund your five dollars," he said to Ryan.

"I appreciate your kind offer," said Mr. Haypence. "But there still remains the problem of what to do with Ryan."

He frowned down at the frightened little boy.

"You realize, Ryan, that you've done something very wrong," he said.

Ryan nodded.

"You've used Hollis to harbor an animal that has destroyed school property. From what I hear, it has disrupted meals in our brand-new lunchroom. Not to mention the fact that it has interrupted a very important volleyball game."

Ryan's chin was starting to tremble.

"At the very least, you deserve to be suspended," Mr. Haypence went on inexorably. "And that is why I have decided to—"

Ryan's face was white.

"—to do nothing," said Mr. Haypence.

"*What?*" gasped Bonnie in relief.

"Nothing," repeated the principal. "I can remember how much I wanted a pet as a boy, and how I wasn't allowed to have one. I would have been a much happier boy if I could have had a hamster of my own."

"You're not going to—you're not going to— oh, thanks!" shrieked Ryan. "Thanks a lot!"

"That's great of you, Mr. Haypence," Bob said happily.

Mr. Haypence was smiling. "Well, you know, some strange things happened, but no one was hurt," he said gently. "Of course, I'm relying on you not to conceal any more pets in school, Ryan."

"Hey, no problem!" Ryan assured him. Then his smile dimmed a little. "I don't have a pet anymore, anyway."

"Could I make a suggestion?" Mr. Vilas said. "Perhaps you'd allow me to donate a hamster to Ryan's class. As a little reward for finding my ferret, you might say."

"Oh, that would be great!" Ryan gasped.

"As long as his teacher thinks it's okay," said Mr. Vilas quickly. "And you, too, of course, Mr. Haypence."

"I think it's an excellent suggestion," Mr. Haypence said with a chuckle. "If the teacher doesn't want the hamster in her classroom, I'll be happy to keep it in my office. And Ryan, you're welcome to visit it as often as you like."

"*Yay!*" Ryan whooped. "I'm going to have my hamster after all!"

Everyone was smiling at everyone else, and Ryan reached up and hugged Bonnie. It seemed as if everything was going to turn out just fine.

"Can I just ask one thing?" called the Brookside principal from her spot in the stands. "I'm glad to see there was a good explanation for all that chaos—but is my raincoat still out in your car, Mr. Vilas?"

Mr. Vilas blanched. "Uh-oh," he said. "Let me run and get it for you. If it's still in one piece," he added under his breath. "I hope my *car* is still in one piece."

Mr. Haypence checked his watch. "Oh, good," he said. "There's plenty of time to resume the game. Bonnie, would you mind calling back the people in the hall while I get the teams from the locker room?"

Bonnie beamed at him. "I'd be delighted to. And while I'm at it, Mr. Haypence, I think I'll join your cheering section, too."